Postman Pat® and the Runaway Kite

SIMON AND SCHUSTER

It was the day of the Greendale kite festival.

Julian had just finished making his kite.

"That's a real smasher, Julian!" said Pat. "Now come on, Jess, time for work."

Jess jumped onto the table to follow Pat . . . and got all tangled up in Julian's kite.

"Oh Jess!" Julian cried. "Mum! Look what he's done! Now it's ruined."

"Never mind, love," said his mother, "there's still time to make a new kite."

Julian cheered up a bit. "I'll see if Charlie can help!"

As Pat and Jess arrived at the Post Office, the wind was blowing leaves everywhere. One landed right on Jess's nose!

Pat laughed. "What a blustery day! Can you see where you're going, Jess?"

Julian and Charlie Pringle were busy making their kites. Charlie was carefully measuring all the angles. "My kite's going to be a super flyer!" he said.

"Mine's a special Pencaster United kite, look!" Julian said proudly.
"It matches my scarf!"

At the station Ajay was polishing the Greendale Rocket.

"What's that weird noise, Dad?" asked Meera.

"It's the wind!" said Ajay. "It's a singing steam engine!"

"That gives me an idea," said Meera. "I wonder if I could make my kite sing. . . ."

Julian and Charlie decided to try out their kites.

Charlie held his kite up. "Hmm. If the angle is just so. . . then the wind speed should push it up even higher."

"Wow! It works! Isn't it amazing?"

"Er, yeah, it's flying well, but doesn't it look a bit . . . boring?" Julian frowned.

"Look at mine!" shouted Julian as his kite finally climbed higher and higher into the sky . . . did a big loop the loop . . . and then crashed back down to the ground.

Julian sighed. "What we need is a kite that looks good, does tricks *and* stays up in the air!"

"I've got it!" cried Charlie. "Let's join our kites together!"

Meanwhile, Pat and Jess were on their way to Ted Glen's. There was a large parcel for him.

"I wonder what Ted's been ordering this time?" chuckled Pat.

It was a packet of ribbon.

"Whatever do you want all that ribbon for?" said Pat.

"It's for my kite," explained Ted. "It makes a champion tail."

Pat was admiring Ted's kite when a gust of wind blew his hat off.
"Don't worry, Pat. We'll catch it!" said Ted.

While Pat and Ted chased after Pat's hat, Jess explored Ted's kite.
Another big gust of wind suddenly whipped it up into the air . . .

taking Jess with it!

"Miaow! Miaow! Miaow!"

"Oh poor Jess!" Pat jumped into his van. "Quick, Ted! Follow that kite!"

But Ted's kite was gathering speed and soon Jess was flying high above the treetops.

Pat and Ted got out of the van.

"By gum, look at him go!" said Ted, as Jess zoomed over the fields.

"Come on, Pat!"

"Don't worry, Jess!" puffed Pat. "We'll catch you!"

A big crowd had gathered on the hilltop.

Ajay welcomed everyone to Greendale's very first kite festival. "Best of luck, and happy flying!"

The sky was suddenly full of beautiful kites. Julian and Charlie's kite soared, and Meera's musical kite jingled through the air.

And there was Jess, flying Ted Glen's kite!

Pat ran up the hill, out of breath.

"Oh Dad! Poor Jess!" cried Julian. "Come on, Charlie, let's loop the loop and get Jess down!"

Charlie and Julian's kite twirled and twisted around Ted's kite.
"OK, everybody," called Pat. "One, two, three, PULL!"

The kites slowly fluttered to the ground, and Jess landed safe and sound.

Pat gave him a big hug. "Welcome back, Jess!"

Jess purred happily.

"Now for the prize-giving!" announced Ajay. "The prize for the prettiest and most musical kite goes to . . . Meera. For the kite with the best flying skills – a trophy for Julian and Charlie . . . and our special prize goes to the bravest kite-flyer – JESS!"

"I reckon we've had enough of flying cats!" laughed Pat.

"Miaow," agreed Jess.

SIMON AND SCHUSTER
First published in 2004 in Great Britain by Simon & Schuster UK Ltd
Africa House, 64-78 Kingsway
London WC2B 6AH
A CBS COMPANY

This hardback edition published in 2007

A CIP catalogue record for this book is available from the British Library upon request

ISBN-10: 1-84738-076-X
ISBN-13: 978-1-84738-076-0

Printed in China
1 3 5 7 9 10 8 6 4 2